E
C.2

Shannon, George
    The Piney Woods peddler. Pictures
by Nancy Tafuri.   Greenwillow, 1981.
    32 p. col. illus.

    I. Title.

50048908   81-2219/11.88/add7

GREENWILLOW
BOOKS
New York

THE PINEY WOODS PEDDLER

TOLD BY
GEORGE SHANNON
PICTURES BY
NANCY TAFURI

Printed in U.S.A.   First Edition
1   2   3   4   5   6   7   8   9   10

Library of Congress Cataloging in Publication Data
Shannon, George.   The Piney Woods peddler.
Summary: A peddler sets out to find a shiny
silver dollar for his dear darling daughter.
[1. Peddlers and peddling – Fiction]
I. Tafuri, Nancy.   II. Title.
PZ7.S5287Pi   [E]   81-2219
ISBN 0-688-80304-0   AACR2
ISBN 0-688-84304-2 (lib. bdg.)

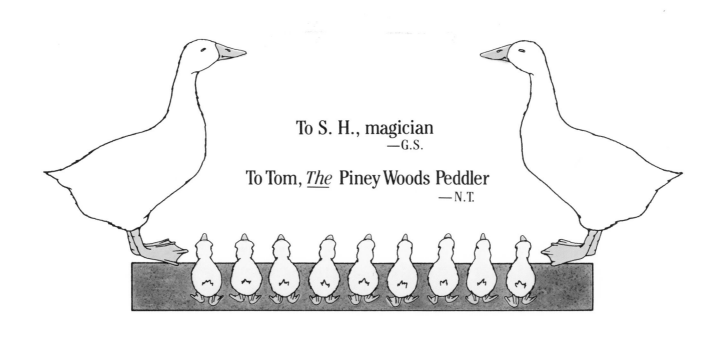

To S. H., magician
—G.S.

To Tom, *The* Piney Woods Peddler
—N.T.

Once, back a ways, lived the Piney Woods peddler. He traveled through the woods and up and down the rivers. Wherever he went, he was swapping and trading. He'd trade anything he had except his dear darling daughter. He loved her more than words can tell.

One day his dear darling daughter said, "Daddy, get me a shiny silver dollar so I can buy some pretty things."

"Yes, indeed," said the peddler, "and soon to boot!"

He hopped on his horse and rode off to find a dollar.

5

The frogs were a-croaking. The birds were a-flying and the peddler was soon a-singing:

"With a wing wang waddle
And a great big straddle
And a Jack-fair-faddle
It's a long way from home."

Before long he met a barefoot woman with a big brown cow. Said the Piney Woods peddler to the barefoot woman:

"Trade you my horse
Trade you my ring
For a shiny silver dollar
I'll trade anything."

Woman said, "Got no shiny silver dollar, but we can trade just the same— my big brown cow for your big black horse." So the Piney Woods peddler swapped his horse for the cow and off he went.

7

The woodpeckers were
a-pecking and the peddler
walked a-singing:

*"With a wing wang waddle
And a great big straddle
And a Jack-fair-faddle
It's a long way from home."*

Now along came a man
with a strong black mule.
Said the Piney Woods
peddler to the strong
mule-man:

"Trade you my cow
Trade you my ring
For a shiny silver dollar
I'll trade anything."

Mule-man said, "Got no
shiny silver dollar, but we
can trade just the same—
my strong black mule
for your big brown cow."
So the Piney Woods
peddler swapped his
cow for the mule.

9

The bees were a-buzzing and the peddler walked a-singing:

"With a wing wang waddle
And a great big straddle
And a Jack-fair-faddle
It's a long way from home."

Soon came a boy with a fine hunting dog.

Said the
Piney Woods peddler
to the hunting-dog boy:

*"Trade you my mule
Trade you my ring
For a shiny silver dollar
I'll trade anything."*

Boy said, "Got no shiny
silver dollar, but we can
trade just the same—
my fine hunting dog for
your strong mule."
So the Piney Woods
peddler swapped his
mule for the dog.

11

The flies were a-flitting
and the peddler walked
a-singing:

*"With a wing wang waddle
And a great big straddle
And a Jack-fair-faddle
It's a long way from home."*

By and by
came a man with a
big wood stick.

Said the Piney Woods
peddler to the
wood-stick man:

*"Trade you my dog
Trade you my ring
For a shiny silver dollar
I'll trade anything."*

The man said, "Got no
shiny silver dollar, but we
can trade just the same—
my big wooden stick for
your fine hunting dog."
So the Piney Woods
peddler swapped his dog
for the stick.

13

The wind was a-whistling and the peddler walked a-singing:

"With a wing wang waddle
And a great big straddle
And a Jack-fair-faddle
It's a long way from home."

Then along came a rattlesnake rattling all his rattlers. Said the Piney Woods peddler to the long rattlesnake:

"Trade you my stick
Trade you my ring
For a shiny silver dollar
I'll trade anything."

Snake said, "Got no shiny silver dollar, but I've got teeth of poison. I'll take your stick instead!"

15

That snake jumped at the stick and bit down hard. His teeth went so deep he couldn't get them out. The peddler didn't worry.

16

He just picked up
that stick and swung it
around and around and
up and down

17

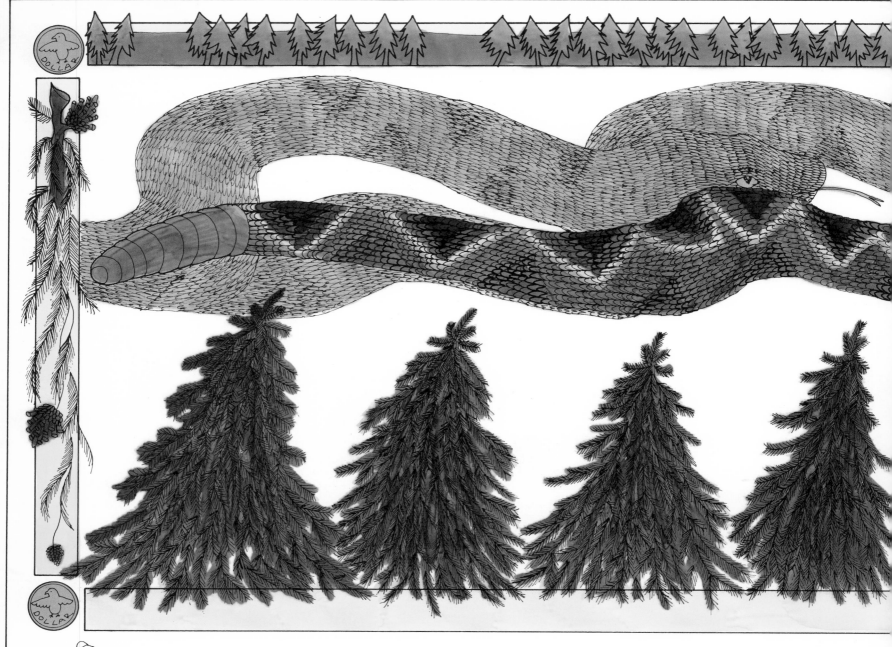

18

till that snake went flying by the trees.

Then the Piney Woods peddler smiled and walked off a-singing:

*"With a wing wang waddle
And a great big straddle
And a Jack-fair-faddle
It's a long way from home."*

Now as he sang, his stick began to swell. The snake's poison was spreading through the wood.

The more the poison worked, the more the stick swelled. It was soon as big as two trees—three trees—four.

21

About this time came a railroad man. Said the Piney Woods peddler to the railroad man:

*"Trade you my stick
Trade you my ring
For a shiny silver dollar
I'll trade anything."*

The man said, "I've got
a shiny silver dollar
and I'd be glad to make
the trade."
"Good," said the peddler,
"I knew I'd get a dollar for
my dear darling daughter.
Here's the stick.
Where's the dollar?"
"Don't have it with me,"
said the man. "Tell you
what I'll do. I'll bring it to
your house tomorrow
before noon."

The peddler walked home
a-singing as happy as
could be:

*"With a wing wang waddle
And a great big straddle
And a Jack-fair-faddle
It's a long way from home."*

The railroad man cut and chopped that stick into three hundred and three strong railroad ties. He was pleased with the trade.

25

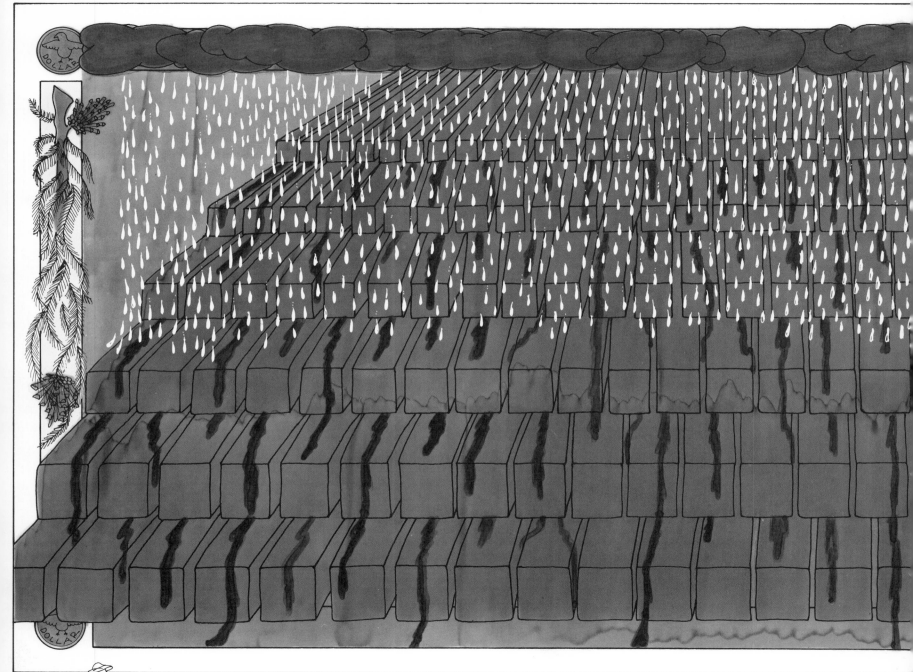

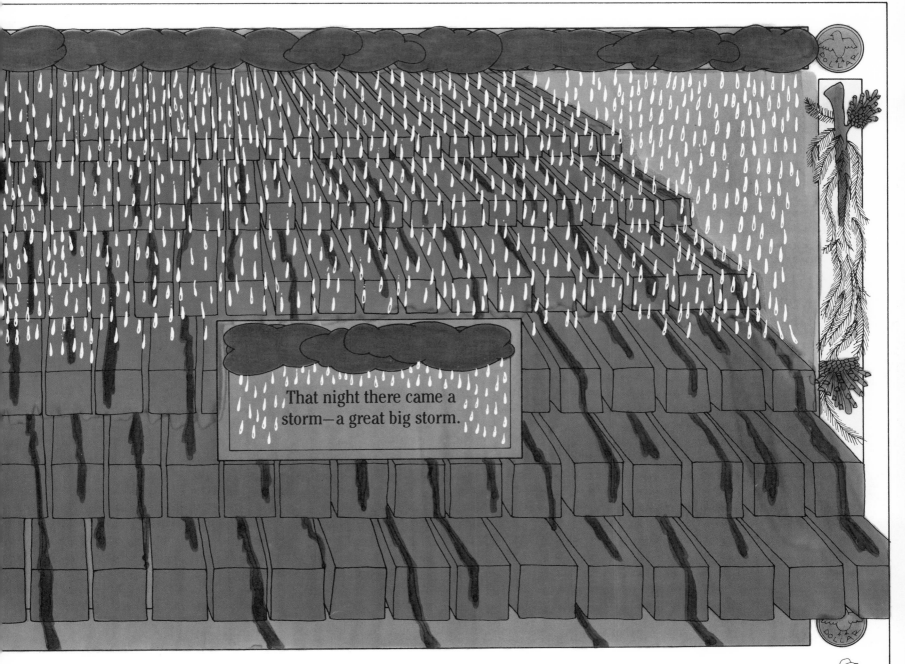

That night there came a
storm—a great big storm.

27

It rained so hard
it washed the poison
out of the wood.
As the poison washed out,
the swelling went down.
Those ties got smaller
and smaller
and smaller still.
When the sun came up,
they were no bigger than
toothpicks.

The railroad man ran
to the peddler's house
way before noon.
"Your stick shrunk down.
It's not worth a dollar.
It's barely worth a dime!"

29

"Let me see that dime!"
cried the dear darling
daughter. She held it to
the light and it shone
like a star. "I like it," said
the daughter. "It's like
a shiny silver dollar, but
dear and darling like me!"
"You can keep it," said
the peddler, "and I'll start
trading again for your
shiny silver dollar."

30

He kissed her goodbye
and set off down the road.
And all the while
he walked, he kept on
a-singing:

31